To Akira

Walter Lorraine Books

Library of Congress Cataloging-in-Publication Data

Van Allsburg, Chris.
    The Z was zapped.

    Summary: Depicts how A was in an avalanche,
B was badly bitten, C was cut to ribbons, and
the other letters of the alphabet suffered
similar mishaps.
    1. Alphabet. I. Title
PZ7.V266Zab   1987   [E]   87-14988
ISBN 0-395-44612-0   PA ISBN 0-395-93748-5

Printed in the United States of America

LBM 20 19 18 17 16 15 14 13 12

THE ALPHABET THEATRE

Proudly Presents

THE Z WAS ZAPPED

A PLAY IN TWENTY-SIX ACTS

PERFORMED BY

THE CASLON PLAYERS

WRITTEN AND DIRECTED BY

MR. CHRIS VAN ALLSBURG

PRODUCED BY

HOUGHTON MIFFLIN COMPANY BOSTON

ACT 1

The A was in an Avalanche.

The B was badly Bitten.

The C was Cut to ribbons.

The D was nearly Drowned.

The E was slowly Evaporating.

The F was firmly Flattened.

The G was starting to Grow.

ACT 8

The H was partly Hidden.

The I was nicely Iced.

The J was rather Jittery.

The K was quietly Kidnapped.

The L was much too Large.

The M was beginning to Melt.

The N was Nailed and Nailed again.

The O was rapidly Overgrown.

The P was repeatedly Pecked.

The Q was neatly Quartered.

The R was Rolled off-stage.

The S was simply Soaked.

The T was all Tied up.

The U was abruptly Uprooted.

The V was mysteriously Vanishing.

The W was oddly Warped.

The X was carefully X-rayed.

The Y was Yanked away.

The Z was finally Zapped.